Snowed In at POKEWEED PUBLIC SCHOOL

By John Bianchi

Every morning, I rush through the house – eating breakfast, combing my wool, brushing my teeth. Then I pack my bag, hug my parents and blast off for the bus. It's time for another classic day at Pokeweed Public School.

I always sit in the front of the bus with my best friend Melody. That way, we can get away from the animals at the back.

When we get off the bus, Ms. Mudwortz is always there to meet us. She's the best teacher in the whole world. We all think she's awesome.

Ms. Mudwortz never gets upset. Whenever we become too noisy or enthusiastic, she just stops whatever she's doing, raises her hoof and waits for us to settle down.

There's always something excellent
going on at Pokeweed Public School.

Like a Hallowe'en Party. . .

or a science fair. . .

or a track meet. . .

BICYCLE
HELMETS
DING

AND YOUR
BRAIN

or a visit from Officer Platz for a talk
about bicycle safety.

But the best day we ever had at Pokeweed Public School happened last week. Ms. Mudwortz had yard duty, and we had just talked her into playing goal when all of a sudden it really started to snow.

In fact, the snow was piling up so fast that Ms. Mudwortz thought the bus should be called to take us home early.

But Principal Slugmeyer was very busy and could not be disturbed. By the time he finished his work, it was the end of the day and we were all. . .

. . . SNOWED IN!

When Principal Slugmeyer announced that we would have to spend the night at school, everyone went totally ballistic.

Some of the younger students started crying for their parents. Some of the older students started cheering and clapping and jumping around. Melody and I just wondered: What would we do? What would we eat? Where would we sleep?

Then good old Ms. Mudwortz calmly took control of the whole situation. First she sent us to the gymnasium with Principal Slugmeyer for a long game of dodge ball. I think they wanted to tire us out. But the only one who got tired. . .

BONK!

. . .was Principal Slugmeyer.

After the game, we were all starting to get hungry. No problem for Ms. Mudwortz. She had gone to the staff room and found enough stuff to whip up a whole bunch of hayburgers and vegetarian pizzas.

When it got dark, Billy wanted to start a fire but Ms. Mudwortz reminded him that, although we were snowed in, the lights and furnace still worked fine. That must have given her an idea. She placed a lamp in the middle of the floor and decorated it like a campfire. Then she got out her guitar, and we all sang songs. Principal Slugmeyer even did his famous spoon solo.

Finally, it was time for bed. We got some mats from the gym and used our coats for blankets. Then Ms. Mudwortz had all the older students read stories to all the younger students.

I read Billy a story about a hummingbird who forgot how to hum and he fell asleep before I finished.

There were lots of weird noises at first, but eventually everyone said their good-nights and settled down. Ms. Mudwortz settled down so fast she fell asleep with her hoof in the air.

By the next morning, the snow had stopped falling, the plow had cleared the roads, and Principal Slugmeyer had shovelled the whole laneway. The bus took us all home, but we didn't get off.

Our parents just handed us a lunch and waved
goodbye. It was already time to go back and have
another classic day at Pokeweed Public School.